청어詩人選 334

# 그곳을 지나가면서
## Passing the Way There

심재황
한영시집

청어

# 그곳을 지나가면서
Passing the Way There

# 쉽고 아름답게

어려운 말이나 복잡한 표현
이해하기 어려워요

예쁜 꽃잎들
따스한 햇살
아름다운 그대 모습
어찌 전달하여 주나요

그건 어렵지 않아요
그냥 쉬운 말로 전해요

그대가 알아듣고 미소 짓게
쉬운 말 쉬운 글이 아름다워요
그대가 그대로 느끼면 아름다워요

# Easy and Beautiful

Hard words or intricate phrases,
Are hard to share and understand.

Pretty petals,
Warm sunlight,
Your beautiful image,
How do I deliver for you?

It's not challenging,
For I'm just saying it in simple words.

For you to understand of it and smile,
Easy words and phrases are beautiful.

When you feel the way they are,
How beautiful they are!

# 차례

## 1부　지나가는 길에서(On the Way There)

## 2부  그리운 것들(The Beloved Ones)

# 3부  다시 지나가는 길에서(On the Way There Again)

# 1부

# 지나가는 길에서
## (On the Way There)

진한 녹색 잎사귀들 사이에서
한 송이는 활짝 퍼져 나왔는데
옆으로 삐져나온 줄기 끝에서
또 한 송이 반쯤이나 벌어졌어요

# 가을비와 색깔

오늘은 화요일 아침인데
11월 마지막 하루이니까
올해 가을도 이제 끝인가 보다

궁내공원 나무들이 젖으니
올해 마지막 가을비인가 보다

지금 내리는 가을비는
지난주 꾸며 놓은 묘소도 적시는데
하얗게 둘러진 조약돌에 흘러내리고
동그랗게 웅크린 꽃잔디에 스며들고

내일 한낮이 되어서
가을 햇살을 받게 된다면
늦가을 색깔을 만들어가겠지

# A Color of Rain in Fall

On Tuesday morning
It's the last day of November.

This fall is going over,
Trees on the park are wetting.

It might be the last rain
In the fall of this year, I guess.

The rain is falling
On the grave trimmed last week,
Flowing down the white pebbles
Around the grave there,
Shedding the curled grass.

Tomorrow afternoon
If sunlight shines on the grave,
It will generate the hues of late fall.

# 수리산 산신각

앙상한 나무들 빼곡한데
양쪽 골짜기에 낙엽이 쌓이고

탁자바위 아래 소나무는
삭아들고 껍질도 벗겨져서
허연 속살이 허전히 드러나네

기울어진 느티나무는
허리를 구부리고 비틀고서
두꺼운 껍질은 이끼로 덮이고

기와지붕 막새마다
마른 잡초 수북하게 자라서
저녁 햇살은 갈색으로 비추네

# A Shrine at Surisan Valley

On both sides of the valley,

Bare trees are abound,

And fallen leaves are piled up.

Under the table rock,

The pine tree is dried out,

The skin is peeled off,

And the empty inside is exposed.

The tilted zelkova

Bending its back and twisted,

The thick bark is covered with moss.

On each tile roof,

Dry weeds grow in abundance,

The evening sun shines in brown.

# 비 내리는 아침

밝은 빛을 바라며 거실 커튼을 거두고
서늘한 공기를 바라며
창문을 열어 보네

발코니 창문은 빗방울에 젖어있으며
낡은 창문 틈새로
빗물이 스며들었네

어제 늦은 밤에는 내리지 않았는데
이른 새벽부터
한동안 내렸나보네

창문을 반쯤 열고 손에 빗물을 적셔서
이마에 살며시 대어보니
코 위로 흘러내리네

손 안에 담아보니 차가운 빗물이니까
이번에 내리는 비는
마지막 가을비인가 보다

# In the Rainy Morning

Hoping for a bright light,
Removing the curtains in the living room,

Hoping for the cool air,
I open the window in my apartment.

The balcony windows are wet with raindrops.
Through the window, rain drops seep in.

It didn't rain last night, but from early morning,
It has been down for a while.

I open the window halfway, wet my hand with the rain,
Put it on my forehead, and it drips down on my
nose.

Putting it in my hand, I feel it's cold rainwater.
This morning, it may be the last rain this fall.

# 사로국 가는 길

해 떠오르는 사로국은 밝게 빛난다는데
서라벌 왕궁은 가을 햇살처럼 빛난다는데
사로국 가는 길은 멀기만 하네

저 멀리 금학산 바라보며
너른 들녘을 천천히 지날 때
쌍계천 억새 숲은 은빛 수실을 흔들었지

양지마을로 내려가고 좁은 길 돌아가니
차가운 얼음골에 다다르게 되겠네

멀리 북두산 봉우리는 줄지어 가파른데
매봉산 돌길을 힘들여 넘어야 한다는데

아미산 저녁 해는 쌍계천 벌판을 비춘다지
사로국 가는 길은 멀기도 하네

# The Road to Seorobeol Kingdom

From the Seorabeol Kingdom, the sun rises.
The palace is bright as autumn sunshine.
But the passage to Seorabeol is a long way.

Looking at Mt. Geumhak in the distance,
Passing slowly through the wide field,
The golden reeds on Ssanggyecheon stream
Wave the silver thread of the leaves.

Going down to the sunny village,
Passing through the narrow path,
Approaching the cold icy valley,
The peak of the Mt. Bukdusan is seen,
The steep peaks and deep valleys are lined up.

Crawling up the stone path of Mt. Maebongsan,
Climbing Mt. Amisan in the evening,
The sun illuminates the plain of Ssanggyecheon.
The passage to Seorabeol is a long way.

# 가을 칼국수 맛

몇 년 전 늦가을인지 초겨울인지
복숭아 농장 벗과 찾아갔던 곳인데
두툼한 손칼국수 한가득 담아주셨죠

무극면 시내 한참 벗어난 시골 마을
작은 골목길 위로 양철지붕 집이죠

생극면 시가지 농협 지나기 전에
한산하던 시외버스 터미널 근처에
그곳 된장찌개도 담백했어요

차평 길가 식당 김치찌개도 칼칼했고
냇가 옆 기사식당 반찬도 담백했어요

어디에라도 가을 길을 가다 보면
가을 맛을 맞추어주네요

# Noodle Broth in Fall

Some years ago, in late fall or early winter,
I visited with a friend of a peach farm.

We tried a dish of thick hand-made noodle broth
At a kitchen-dining room with a tin roof.

Some years ago, passing the bank downtown,
Near the busy intercity bus terminal,
The soybean paste stew was also appealing.

The kimchi stew at another roadside restaurant
Was a little hot and spicy.

The side dishes was fresh and flavorsome
At a driver's restaurant next to the stream.

Wherever you go on a road in fall,
It reflects us the relish of fall.

# 덕천마을에서 차 마시고

덕천마을 선생님께서는
차를 내려주시는데
연한 단풍나무 색깔이어서

황토 담장에 드리워진
늦가을 햇살이
은근히 비추고 있어요

덕천마을 선생님께서는
차를 내려주시는데
밝은 갈참나무 색깔이어서

담장 아래 아담하게 피어난
노란 국화 향기가
차분히 스며들어 있어요

# Drinking Tea at Deokcheon Village

The green tea

By the master madame at Deokcheon Village

Is a light maple color

Along the ocher wall

Of late autumn sunlight.

The green tea

By the master madame at Deokcheon Village

Is a bright oak color

In the fade garden

Of late autumn sunlight

The green tea

Is bearing yellow chrysanthemum scent

Blooming quietly under the wall.

# 동백 두 송이

벌써 12월 두 번째 목요일에
산 너머 바닷바람 때문인지

한밤에 달빛이 너무나 차가운지
새빨간 동백꽃 두 송이 피었어요

진한 녹색 잎사귀들 사이에서
한 송이는 활짝 퍼져 나왔는데
옆으로 삐져나온 줄기 끝에서
또 한 송이 반쯤이나 벌어졌어요

여남은 작은 봉오리들은
붉은 빛깔을 살짝 띠고서는
꽃덮개 안에서 단단히 숨어있어요

다음 주에 며칠 추워진다고 하니까
몇 송이가 더 붉게 터져 나오겠어요

# Two Pieces of Camellias

On the second Thursday in early December,
Because of the sea breeze over the hill,
Because of bright moonlight at night,
Two bright red camellias bloomed.

One spread out among dark green leaves.
Another bud is half open at a stem tip
Protruding from the side of a stem.

The remaining small buds with reddish tint
Are hidden inside the flower petals.

After cold for a few days next week,
And a few more will burst out in red.

# 참깨밭 남은 자국

참깨밭 고랑은 흐트러졌지만
바쁘게 오가던 자국은 남아있어요

농부의 장화 자국이 길게 찍혀있고
경운기 바퀴 자국도 깊이 박혀있고
베어진 줄기 밑동아리 줄지어 있어요

작은 밭고랑 밑동아리는
아침 햇살 비출 무렵부터
한가하게 낫으로 베어내서
선명하게 날 선 자국인데

넓은 밭고랑 밑동아리는
저녁 해 질 무렵이 되니까
서둘러 예초기로 베어내서
거칠고 무딘 자국입니다

# The Traces of Sesame Field

The sesame furrow was littered,
The traces where busy farmers worked
Still remain there.

The long prints of the farmer's boots,
The marks of cultivator wheels
Are deeply embedded.

The stems cut off are lined up in the field.

The bottom of small furrow
Is the traces of cutting off
Leisurely with a sickle
By farmers in the early morning.

However, the bottoms of wide furrow
Is the traces of cutting off
With a machine trimmer
Hurrying up late in the afternoon.

# 옹달샘에 낙엽 떨어지고

가을 햇살은 드세지 않은데
하늘을 뒤덮었던 잎사귀는
참나무 떡갈나무에서 떨어져 날려요

골짜기에 여러 겹이나 쌓이다가
흐트러진 바위 틈새를 막아버렸어요

바위 사이로 샘물이 스며서 나오다가
낙엽에 막혀서 옹달샘을 이루었어요

옹달샘은 할 수 없이
젖은 낙엽을 담아두고
아쉬운 햇살마저도 담아두려는데

가을 하늘 햇살은
찬물에 놀라서 튕겨 나가고
젖은 낙엽만이 눈부시게 담겨있어요

# Fallen Leaves in a Small Spring

The sun is not shining;
The leaves that covered the sky
Fallen from an oak tree and blown it away.

The Leaves stacked up layers in the valley,
Closed the cracks in the loose rocks.

A water seeps through the rocks,
Clogged with fallen leaves forming a spring.

The spring tries to keep wet leaves,
Contains even weak sunlight in it.

The sunlight, however, is startled
By the cold water, bounces off.

Only wet leaves are dazzling
In the spring in a quiet valley.

# 낙엽송 오솔길

새벽에 차가운 공기가
낙엽송 사이에 스며들어서

떨어진 바늘잎은
산길에 수북이 쌓였어요

한밤에 산속 짐승들은
관목 수풀을 헤치고 밟아서

떨어진 낙엽송 사이에
오솔길을 만들었어요

다음 날 낯선 등산객들도
둘레길 오르고 내려가면서

떨어진 낙엽송 사이에
오솔길을 만들었어요

# A Larch Path

Cold air in the early morning
Is seeping among the larch,
Fallen needle leaves
Are piled up
On the path in the forest.

At midnight,
The animals of the forest
Treading through the shrubbery
Made a path among the larch.

The next day,
Strangers in the forest
Going up and down the roundabout
Made a path among the larch.

# 첫눈을 기다리나

다음 주에는
눈이 내린다는데
첫눈을 기다려야 하나

그날 저녁에는
첫눈이 내리는 날에
여기로 온다고 했는데

그날 만나게 되면
첫눈이 내리는 날에
무슨 말을 하려나 본데

무슨 말을 기대해야 하나
첫눈을 기다려야 하는데
무슨 말을 기대해야 하나

# Waiting for the First Snow

Next week
It will be snowing.
Should I wait for the first snow?

In the evening
Of the first snow
Someone will be coming here.

On the day
Because of the first snow
Someone will try to say something.

For the meeting
Between you and me
Should I wait for the first snow?
Should I wait for any words?

# 사이봉 오르는 길

사이봉 오르는 길은
가파른 경사로 굽을 수밖에 없는데

붉은 소나무 무리는
비탈에 의지하니 나이보다 작아 보여요

가는 나무 둘레는
겨우 한 뼘 반 정도인데
굵은 나무 둘레는
다섯 뼘이나 되겠어요

하지만 솟아오른 높이는
가는 나무 굵은 나무 모두 마찬가지

한겨울에 되어서는
남서쪽 햇빛을 넉넉히 받으며
가지마다 흰 눈을 수북이 담겠어요

# A Steep Path to Saibong Peak

Because of the steep hillside,
The path to Saibong peak is curved and bended.

Growing up on the slope,
The red pines don't tall for their age, and
The waist is only about a span and a half.

The thick trees, however,
Are at most around three spans.

Yet the height soaring to the sky
Is almost the same as thin and thick trees.

In the middle of winter,
With sunlight from the southwest,
The trees will hold plenty of white snow
On the branches and leaves.

# 칼바위 소나무

삐져나온 철쭉 뿌리를 디디면서
한 굽이 오르고

갈참나무 가지를 부여잡아 끌면서
한 굽이 오르고

늙은 참나무 줄기에 등을 기대고서
한 굽이 올라보니

하얀 차돌이 부서지고 깨져서
칼날을 드러내는데

돌 틈을 비집고 솟아난 붉은 소나무는
휘어진 우산처럼 날개 펼치고서
칼바위 아래 낭떠러지를 내려다보네요

# A Pine Tree on Kalbawi Rock

Stepping on the protruding azalea roots

One step goes up.

Grabbing the oak branches

And dragging them

One step goes up.

Leaning back against the trunk

Of an old oak tree

I climb up the curved trail.

The red pine tree

Rising from Kalbawi Rock

Spreads its wings like an umbrella,

Looking down the cliff.

# 늦가을 찬바람

이제 가을도 깊어가기에
찬바람 불어오겠는데

늦가을 찬바람은
형제봉 아래 여우고개 넘어서

깊어진 소류지 둑을 건너서
감나무골로 불어오겠지

한겨울에 함박눈은
굳건한 장군바위 넘어서

낮은 고라니 샛길 지나고
버섯마을로 내려와서는
밭길까지 덮어버리겠지

# Cold Wind in Late Fall

Now that fall is deepening
A cold wind will blow.

The cold wind in late fall
Over the narrow Fox Path
Under the Hyeongjebong Peak
Crossing the deepened Soryuji Bank
Will blow to the persimmon tree of the village.

The snow in the middle of winter
Beyond the huge General Rock,
Passing through the low hill,
Will reach Mushroom Village
And at last cover the bare field.

# 그분은 떠나가고

그분은 떠나가도
나누던 추억은 남아있겠지요

그분이 떠나기에
나누던 추억은 더 아름다울까요

그런데 아름다운 추억은
어쩐지 슬픔으로 남아있네요

그분은 떠나가면서
함께 나누던 추억을
슬픔으로 남겨놓았어요
외로움으로 남겨놓았어요

# After You Leave

After you leave,
The memories we have shared
Will remain between us.

Because you leave,
The memories will be more beautiful.

But the beautiful memories with you
Will remain somehow sad.

Because you leave,
The memories with you
Still leave me with sadness,
Still leave me with loneliness.

# 진눈깨비

가랑비 내리는가 했는데
이내 진눈깨비가 내리네

산에서 내려온 진눈깨비는
밭둑을 따라가면서 적시네

대추나무도 적시고
배나무 봉오리도 젖어들고
진흙 담장도 진하게 젖어드네

바로 이곳으로 내려와서
모과나무도 줄기도 적시고
말라붙은 코스모스도 젖어드네

# The Sleet in Fall

It may be raining;
However, it's getting sleet soon.

The sleet comes down from the forest,
Wets and runs along the bank of a field.

It wets jujube trees along the bank,
Pear buds in the orchard,
And the mud wall of all huts in the village.

Coming down right here,
It wets the stem of a quince tree,
And a bundle of faded cosmoses.

# 가을 산책길

가을에 걷는 길은 조용하기만 합니다

봄을 장식하는 산수유, 개나리 색깔이
얼마나 차이가 나는지
살피지 않아도 되지요

진달래, 철쭉, 산벚은 얼마나 화려한지
살피지 않아도 되지요

이팝나무 조팝나무는 순서가 같은지 다른지
살피지 않아도 되지요

가을 산책길에서는
갈색 나뭇잎들만 쌓여 있어서
바스락 바스락 소리는 들려요

갈참나무 옆 바위에 앉더라도
나무줄기 사이로 서늘한 바람이 빠져나와요

# A Walking Path in Autumn

The walking path in autumn is quiet and still.
You don't have to tell the difference of color
Between cornelian cherry and forsythia
Decorating spring season.

You don't have to tell the brightness of flowers
Between wild cherry and azalea in the forest.

You don't have to watch the order of blooming
Among fringe tree, spirea, and so on.

In a walking path in autumn,
Only brown leaves are piled up,
I can hear a little sound of rustling,

When I sit on the rock next to an oak tree,
Only cool wind blows out
Through the trees in the valley.

# 회색 감나무

여름에 무성하던 감나무
가을에 상처가 드러났어요

감나무 가지는 엉겨지고
감나무 기둥은 벌어지고

감나무 껍질은 파여지고
감나무 밑동은 삭아지고

잔가지에 매달려 견디던
시든 연시마저 떨어졌어요

여러 해 견디던 감나무는
가을에 상처를 내보이네요

# A Gray Persimmon Tree

The persimmon tree flourishing in summer
Now exposes scars in fall.

The branches are tangled,
The trunks are peeled open.

The persimmon bark is cut,
The parts of root are dying.

The faded fruits hanging from twigs
Have already fallen at last.

The old tree standing for many years
Only reveals its grey scars late in fall.

# 붉은 사과

주왕산이라고 말하지 않더라도
주산 저수지 안개에 씻기고

매봉산이라고 말하지 않더라도
부남들 따가운 햇살을 받아서

얼음계곡이라고 말하지 않더라도
주산천 맑은 냇물을 마셔서

먼 산봉우리 아래에도
작은 뒷산 언덕 아래에도
줄줄 매달린 붉은 열매뿐이네

주왕산 오가는 길가에도
얼음계곡 넘어가는 길가에도
용천 냇가 따라가는 둑길에도
줄지어 매달린 붉은 사과뿐이네

# Red Apples in the Field

You don't say they're from Mt. Juwangsan,
They are washed in the mist of Jusan Reservoir.

You don't say they're from Mt. Maebongsan,
They receive the warm sunlight in Bunam field.

Though you don't say they're from Ice Valley,
They soak the clear stream of Jusancheon.

Even beneath the distant mountain buds,
Even at the bottom of a small hill behind,
There are only red fruits hanging in rows.

On the road to and from the mountain,
On the side of the road crossing the valley,
On the causeway along the stream,
The fields are covered with red apples
Hanging in a row in fall.

# 2부

## 그리운 것들

### (The Beloved Ones)

눈처럼 하얀 할머니도 지나가네
휴지 담은 수레를 이끌고서
함박눈을 맞으면서
함박눈을 밟으면서

# 반지하 창문과 함박눈

반지하 작은 창문 틈으로
함박눈이 보이네

오전 내내 차가웠는데
저녁까지 기다렸는데
이제 함박눈이 내리네

함박눈이 내린다면
누군가 온다고 했는데
반지하 창문으로 누군가 지나가네

길고양이 한 마리 뛰어가고
강아지 한 마리 쫓아가는데

눈처럼 하얀 할머니도 지나가네
휴지 담은 수레를 이끌고서
함박눈을 맞으면서
함박눈을 밟으면서

# Snow by a Semi-basement Window

Through a small semi-basement window,
I can see falling snowflakes.
It was cold all morning,
And I have been waiting until evening,
It's snowing heavily.

If the snow is coming down in large flakes,
Through the semi-underground window,
Someone is also coming.

Someone is passing,
A stray cat is running,
And a dog is chasing it.

An old woman with white hair passes by,
Leading a cart full of rubbish paper
With stepping on the snow
In the snow flakes.

# 산책길의 친구들

이제 눈발이 날리기 시작하네요

그동안 친구들이 다니던 산길에
발자국도 하얀 눈으로 덮이겠어요

먼저 가신 친구들이 잊으라고
남아 있는 친구들께 이별하네요

저쪽 산길로 가고 있어요
날리는 눈송이 맞으면서
눈길을 밟으며 가네요

어디로 가는지
조용히 걸어가고 있네요

저 멀리 산길인데
눈을 맞으며 가고 있어요

# Friends on a Trail

Now it's starting to snow,
And the mountain trail
Where my friends used to go
Will be covered with white snow.

Even the footprints of my friends
Which they used to leave
Will be covered with white snow.

The friends who passed away before
May farewell to the remaining friends.

They may go down the trail
Quietly in the falling snow.

They are stepping on the snow
Far away into the snow in the path.

# 따스한 차를 마시며

차가운 바람이 불면
따스한 차를 마셔요

은행잎 떨어져 쌓이고
따스한 차를 마셔요

눈마저 내려시 쌓이면
따스한 차를 마셔요

그리운 분들이 생각나서
가을에 떠난 분들 생각하며
따스한 차를 마셔요

따스한 차를 마시면
가을에 떠난 분들이 생각나요

# Drinking Warm Tea

When the cold wind blows,
I drink warm tea.

When ginkgo leaves fall and pile up,
I drink warm tea.

When snow falls and covers the ground,
I drink warm tea.

Remembering of those who left in the fall,
Missing the memories of the fall,
I drink warm tea.

While drinking a warm tea,
I think of a person passing away in fall.

# 첫눈을 걱정하며

기다리던 하얀 첫눈이건만
왜 이렇게 함박 쏟아지는지

왜 이렇게 그치지도 않는지
왜 이렇게 눈바람은 드센지

연립주택 창문에 끼어든 서리를
작은 손으로 살짝 쓸어내리면서
다영이의 걱정은 점점 커져만 가네요

숲 속에 남겨진 고라니는 외로울 텐데
마을버스 타고 가신 엄마는 손이 시릴 텐데
오토바이 배달하는 아빠는 미끄러질 텐데

함박 쏟아지는 첫눈을 보면서
어린 다영이는 아무 말 없다가
이내 눈물을 머금어요

# Watching the First Snow

The first white snow is heavily falling in the air.
Why is it pouring out like this?
Why doesn't it stop like this?
Why is the snow wind so strong?

In the window of the townhouse,
Gently sweeping frost with her small hand,
A child, Dayoung's worries are getting bigger.

A water deer left in the snow forest
Would be lonely.
Mother who went on the town bus
May shiver with cold.
What if the dad driving a motorcycle for delivery
Would slip down on the snow?

Watching the first snow pouring down,
Without a word, a child sheds her tears.

# 등산길 걷던 친구들

이제 산길 오르기는 그만두어야겠지

지쳐서 머뭇거릴 때
손잡아 주던 친구는
무더운 여름날에 멀리 떠났어요
수리골 터널 지나서 화성 함백산 안으로

산 아래 쉼터에서
다정히 웃어주던 친구는
파란 가을날에 멀리 떠났어요
백운산 줄기 한참 지나서 수원 광교산 아래로

산마루 바위에서
시원한 생수 건네주던 친구는
추워진 초겨울에 멀리 떠났어요
청계산 하오고개 넘고 광주 오포골 문형산 자락으로

# The Trails with Friends

Now I have to stop walking mountain trails
Because they passed away.

When I'm tired and left behind the trail,
The friend who held my hand
Went away on a hot summer day
Past the Surigol tunnel to Hwaseong
At the shelter under the mountain.

The friend who smiled kindly on the trail,
Went away on a blue autumn day
Passing by the stem of Gwanggyosan to Suweon.

The friend who handed me a bottle of cold water
Went away in the cold early winter
Across an uphill pass of Cheonggyesan,
At the foot of Munhyeongsan in Opogol, Gwangju.

# 내일 내리는 눈

저녁까지 휘날리던 소나기 눈발이
내일 새벽에 다시 쏟아진다니
얼마나 내리는지 기다려야지

밤나무 산길에 덮이는지
오리나무 숲도 덮이는지
꽃잔디 무덤도 덮이는지

아로니아 심어진 텃밭도
어머니가 빨래 널던 마당도
며칠 동안 눈부시게 보이겠네요

# Snow Tomorrow

The rain and snow fluttered until evening
Will be again tomorrow morning.

I'll have to wait how much and how long
It will fall tomorrow.

Will it cover the chestnut trail?
Will it cover the alder forest?
Will it cover the tomb of moss pink?

The field full of aronia trees
Will look white for a few days.

The yard where my mother hung the laundry
Will look white bright for a time being.

# 낙숫물 보면서

하얗게 쌓인 눈이
하얀 빛을 받아서인지
총총 떨어지고 있네요

한 방울 떨어져서
동백나무 잎사귀에 튀겨 나가고

한 방울 떨어져서
하얀 내 손바닥에 튀겨 나가고

한 방울은 흐르다가
잠시 추위에 멈추어 있더니
고드름으로 달려있네요

# Dripping Roof Water

The white snow on the roof
Reflecting the sunlight
Is falling down drop by drop.

One drop falls on camellia leaves
Scattering over the air.

Another drop falls on a white palm
Scattering over the air.

A third drop falling from the roof
Stops with cold in the air,
Finally makes an icicle from the eaves.

# 크리스마스트리

이번 주에는
옹정리 터골 집에 가서
크리스마스트리를 꾸며놓아야지

마루 문 옆에
하얀 창가 아래에다가
노간주 나무줄기를 꽂아두고는

은빛 수실을 얼기설기 엮어놓고서
은방울 금방울 줄줄이 달아놓으면

어두운 한밤에라도
빨간 별도 반짝이고
노란 별도 반짝이겠지

한겨울에라도 오두막은
이제 아무도 안 계시지만
크리스마스트리가 지키고 있겠지

# A Christmas Tree in a Hut

This week
In the hut of my country,
I will decorate a Christmas tree.

Next to the floor door
Under the small window,
I will put a juniper trunk.

On the branchy tree
I will tangle silver threads,
Hanging golden bright drops.

In the dark night
The red stars will twinkle,
The yellow stars will twinkle.

In the middle of winter
There's no one in the hut;
A Christmas tree will stay there.

# 동백꽃 봉오리

다물어진 동백꽃 봉오리는
무슨 이야기를 담고 있기에
연하게 붉은 색깔을
살짝 내비치면서

어제 아침에도 그대로
오늘 아침에도 그대로

담겨진 빨간 비밀을
이야기 하고플 때가 된다면

다물어진 봉오리를
살짝 터트리고 퍼지겠지

# A Closed Camellia Bud

A closed bud of a camellia

Implies a story,

Slightly reveling a light reddish color.


Same as yesterday morning

Same as this morning

It keeps the hidden red secret.


When she hopes to talk,

When she feels like telling the secret,

The bud will quietly open her lips

And spread her story.

# 관모쉼터 골바람

서쪽 샛길에는
갈색 잎 빛나는데

동쪽 계곡에서
골바람 올라와서는

솔잎을 흔들면서
샛길로 가랑잎을 넘기네요

태을봉 능선 따라서
가느다란 소나무 줄 서 있고

소나무 줄기줄기 사이로
햇살이 비스듬히 비추네요

# Valley Breeze from Gwanmo Ridge

While brown leaves shine
In the eastern valley,
A breeze blows
From the west side valley,

While shaking the pine needles,
The breeze turns over the leaves.

Along the Taeulbong ridge,
Slender pine trees are lined up;
Through the pine trunks,
The sun is shining brightly.

# 고사리 길


썩은 나무 등걸이 축축하고
고사리 길에 낙엽도 촉촉하니

그저께 눈이 내렸다가
어제쯤 눈이 녹았나 보다

드러난 검게 젖은 길바닥에
듬성듬성 발자국 남아있으니

어제 밤이나 이른 새벽에
고라니가 지나갔나 보다

딱따구리가 썩은 나무를 찍을 때
고라니가 홀로 지나갔나 보다

# The Fern Path

Rotten wood stumps get wet,
Even the leaves of the fern path are moist.
It snowed the day before yesterday,
But it might melt yesterday.

On a wet, dark, narrow path,
There are still small footprints left.

Last night or early in the morning,
A water deer may have passed.

When a woodpecker pecked a rotten tree,
A water deer may have passed alone.

# 할머니와 동지팥죽

동짓날에는 새벽도 컴컴한데
할머니는 아궁이에 불을 지피고

어제 불려둔 붉은 팥 한 사발을
하얀 찹쌀 한 바가지에 섞어서
작은 가마솥에 부어서 끓이시고

어제 빚어둔 찹쌀 경단 넣어서
저으며 저으며 펄펄 끓이다가
소금 반 숟가락 슬쩍 뿌리셨지

이른 아침에 어두움이 가시고
동산 햇살이 감나무에 비출 때

뜨거워서 김 오르는 팥죽을
하얀 사발에 반쯤 담아서는
작은 소반 위에 올려주셨지

# Grandma and Red Bean Porridge

Before dawn on the cold winter day,
Grandma lights a fire in her furnace.

She took a bowl of soaked red beans,
Mixes it with a bowl of white glutinous rice,
Pours into a small cauldron
And brings to a boil.

She puts the glutinous rice dumplings
That she brushed yesterday.
She stirs and stirs and boils it,
And sprinkles a half spoon of salt.

Early in the morning, the darkness is gone.
When the sun shines on the persimmon tree,
Red bean porridge is hot and steaming.

Grandma put the hot red porridge
In a white bowl on a small platter.

# 뜨끈한 소 여물죽

풀벌레 소리도 잠잠하니
밤마다 안개가 드리우고
새벽에는 찬 서리가 내리네

아직 어두움이 가시지 않았는데
외양간 누렁소가 몸을 휙 흔들면
깔아둔 지푸라기는 푸석거리고

거친 숨소리 푸욱 푸욱 몰아쉬면
입 언저리에 허연 김이 서려드네

갑자기 부르르 등을 떨고서는
큰 눈방올 껌벅 껌벅거리고

우걱 우걱 되새김질하면서
뜨끈한 여물죽을 기다리지요

# Hot Porridge for Cow

The sound of grasshoppers is still,
There is a fog every night and
A cold frost early in the morning.

The darkness has not yet gone;
Whenever a yellow cow shakes its body,
The laid straw is crumbling, crumbling
In a dim stable.

The cow takes a deep breath,
The harsh sound trembles the air,
Grey steam is forming on its mouth.

Suddenly the cow shakes its back,
Glancing over the stable with round eyes.

The cow keeps on chewing the cud,
Waiting for the warm morning porridge.

# 동짓날 팥죽

아침부터 생각하는 이미지는
동지팥죽 한 사발

이달 초에는 친구 어머니께서
동치미 한 단지 보내주셨어요

날이 풀리면 시장에 들러서
팥죽 그리고 시루떡 세 겹 사야지

그런데 올해는 누구에게 드려야 하나요

뜨거운 동지팥죽
시원한 겨울 동치미
쫀득한 팥 시루떡

올해는 드실 분이 안 계시네요

# Red Bean Porridge in Winter

The images in the morning is
A bowl of red bean porridge
For the coldest winter day.

Earlier this month, my friend's mother
Sent me a jar of radish water kimchi.

When the sun goes up,
I will go to the food market nearby,
And buy layers of red bean rice cake.

However, who should I treat to this year?
Hot red bean porridge, cool radish water kimchi,
And chewy red bean rice cake.

No one takes them this year.

# 산이 보이네

가을 낙엽으로 깔렸지만
산이 보이네

산길 아래 바람고개로
산이 보이네

수리사 가파른 비탈에도
산이 보이네

마른 나무 나무 사이로는
저쪽 능선이 보이고

슬기봉 내려진 바위 사이로
가려진 소나무도 보이네

등산객은 보이지 않더라도
가을에는 산이 보이네

# I Can See a Mountain

Though it is covered with autumn leaves,
I can see a mountain.

Through the mountain trail to the wind path,
I can see a mountain.

Even on a steep slope of Surisa temple,
I can see a mountain.

Through the dry trees and thick shrubs,
I can see the ridge over there.

Among the rocks of Seulgibong peak,
I can see the hidden pine grove.

Though no one is seen at the trail,
I can see a mountain in autumn.

# 시루떡 전해드리기

올해 동짓날을 그래도 포근하네요
그런데 시루떡을 준비하지 못했어요

복사골 벗에게 미안합니다
곡차와 곁들여 드시지 못하겠네요

범박골 사모님에게도 미안합니다
아이들 간식이던 시루떡 드리지 못해요
언니 댁에도 나누어 드리지 못하겠네요

공세마을 어르신들께도 죄송합니다
시루떡 꾸러미를 가져가지 못하네요

올해는 시루떡을 마련하지 못했어요
어머니는 방앗간에 주문하지 않았어요

내년에도 시루떡을 드리지 못해요
이제 어머니는 안 계시니까요
작년 늦가을에 가셨으니까요

# Delivering Rice Cake

The winter solstice this year is still cozy.
But I can't prepare rice cake for the day.

I'm sorry for my friend who used to eat it
As a side dish for drinking.
I can't present the cake this year.

I'm also sorry for the ma'am in Beombakgol.
I can't give you rice cake, a snack for children.

I can't even share it with my sister.
I am sorry to the elders of Gongse Village.

I couldn't prepare rice cake this year,
For my mother didn't order it from a mill.

I won't be able to serve rice cake next year,
'Cause she passed away late fall last year.
She is not with me anymore.

# 3부

# 다시 지나가는 길에서
## (On the Way There Again)

그대는 알 수 있나요

잠자리는 어디로 날아가는지
기러기는 어디에서 날아오는지

# 어두운 동지 밤

동지 밤은
언제나 어두웠는지
많은 별은 어디로 가버렸나

동지 밤은
별들도 없어서인지
어두운 밤은 싸늘하기만 하네

밤새도록
싸늘하고 싸늘해도
산꼭대기에서 찬 서리 내려와도

길가 매실 꽃눈은
조용하게 견뎌내겠지
2월에 계곡물이 녹을 때까지

# The Dark Winter Solstice Night

On winter solstice night,

It was always dark, and

Where on earth have all the stars gone?

On winter solstice night,

Because there might be no stars

Dark night is more cold through the night.

Though it's getting more cold,

Cold frost comes down from the peak.

The plum buds on the roadside

Will endure the cold quietly

Until the valley melts in February.

# 고구마 줄기

그대는 알 수 있나요

한여름 장대비 쏟아지면
고구마 줄기로 뒤덮이는지

귀뚜라미 소리 들릴 무렵
너른 밭 덩굴은 사그라지는지

과수나무 가지는 앙상하고
코스모스 씨앗 흐트러지는지

그대는 알 수 있나요

잠자리는 어디로 날아가는지
기러기는 어디에서 날아오는지

# The Sweet Potato Stalks

Can you know it?

When it rains in midsummer,

Why is it covered with sweet potato stalks?

When you hear crickets,

Will the vines in the broad field fade?

Why are the branches of fruit tree bare?

Why is the cosmos seed disheveled?

Can you know it?

Where do dragonflies go?

Where do geese come from in fall?

# 강아지 산책

하얀 강아지는 산책을 나왔어요
추운 겨울이 궁금해서
이리 저리 살펴보면서
총총 걷다가 뛰어가요

하얀 강아지는 춥지 않은가 봐요
따스한 실내에 있었기에
눈길을 뒤척거리면서도
총총충 구르다가 달려요

송이는 강아지 줄을 잡고서
서너 걸음 뒤에서 끌려가요

하얀 강아지는 뒤돌아보면서
발을 힘써 내딛으며 재촉하지만

송이는 모자를 눌러 쓰고서
강아지 발자국만 졸졸 따라가요

# A Dog Walking Around

A white puppy goes out for a walk
Being curious about the cold winter,
Looking around here and there,
Walking and running around.

The white puppy may not feel cold
Having stayed in a warm room,
And rolling itself and running.

Songhi, a little girl, is holding the leash
Being pulled by the puppy
Behind three or four steps.

The white puppy is looking back
And trying itself to go forward.

The little girl follows the puppy,
Pressing her hat on.

# 추운 사철나무

아침에 보았던 사철나무는
얼어붙어서 움직이지 못하고

매일마다 한낮에
잠시 햇살을 받았어도
잎사귀는 그대로 있기는 해도
저녁까지 얼어붙은 초록이네

오늘 밤에도
다시 한파 불어와도
냉기를 뒤집어 쓰고도 견디겠지

그래서 초록 사철나무이겠지
사계절을 견뎌낼 수 있으니까

# A Cold Cedar

The cedar I saw in the morning
Looked frozen and didn't move.

In the middle of the day,
It got some sunlight for a while.
And the leaves still remain
With frozen green till evening.

In cold air tonight,
Even the cold wave blows again,
It'll keep the leaves from harsh air.

So it must be a green cedar tree
Because it can endure the season.

# 겨울에 갈 곳은

겨울이 오면서
한파가 일주일이나 내려앉으니
이제 갈 곳이 없겠어요

산길은 여전히 보이지만
강추위에 바람마저 매서우니
산속 길에 들어서기 망설여져요

문득 남쪽을 바라보며
한겨울 벗이 궁금해지네요
그곳 농장에는 무슨 일이 있을까

어차피 내려간다고 말했으니
함께 거닐며 소식이나 들어볼까
농장에는 무슨 겨울이야기 있는지

# Where to Go in Winter

As winter comes from the north,
The cold wave lasts for a week,
I have nowhere to go right now.

The mountain is still visible,
But the wind is bitter in the cold,
I hesitate to enter the frozen trail.

Suddenly looking out of the window,
A friend of winter occurs to me.
What's going on on his farm?

I've said I would go down someday.
Shall we walk together on the farm?
Shall I hear his news, good or not?
What winter stories have carried there?

# 밝은 불빛

이제는 밝은 불빛이 좋다

넓은 바닷가는 아니더라도
멀리 떨어진 시골은 아니더라도

작은 불빛이라도 비추어진다면
작지만 밝은 불빛으로 모아지니까

밝은 불빛에서 책을 읽으며
오늘 근심 걱정을 잊게 되기를

밝은 불빛에서 나를 읽으며
우울한 분위기에서 벗어나기를

# A Fine Light

Now the bright light is good
Though it's not a wide beach,
Nor far away in the countryside.

Though a small light shines,
It may becomes a bright light
Gathering a small pieces of light.

Reading a book in a bright light,
I will forget my wondering today.

Reading myself in a bright light,
I will escape from a gloomy mood.

# 어느 해맞이

그때 새벽은 상당히 추웠는데
한 명 한 명 산 입구에 모이더니
두 명 세 명씩 손을 잡고서

어두운 산길을 겨우 더듬어서
산꼭대기를 향해 올랐어요

저곳에 오르게 되면
해 뜰 무렵이 되기에
추위는 사그러진다고 하면서

산 능선이 서서히 보이면서
갑자기 햇살이 솟아오르더니
즐거운 얼굴은 붉게 물들었지

내년에도 함께 오자고 하면서
오래도록 해맞이 오자고 했는데
이제는 그때 미소만 남게 되었지

# A Greeting of Sunrise

It was quite cold at dawn.

We gathered at the gate of the mountain.

Two or three groups holding hands,

We barely traced the dark mountain trail,

Climbed the top of the mountain.

We went up climbing hand in hand,

Saying that the cold will fade away

When we get up there and where the sun rises.

As the ridge gradually became visible,

Suddenly the sun came up and faces were dyed red.

Greeting the sunrise at the peak,

We said we would come together next year,

The sun will greet us whenever we meet.

Now all that is left was a smile.

# 가는 길에서

올해도 가야 하는 길인데
어느 길로 어느 쪽으로 가야 하나

그 길로 가는데
화나는 일 없기를

그 길로 가는데
안타까움이 없기를

그 길로 가는데
애처로움이 없기를

그 길로 가다가 누구를 만나게 될까

서로 사랑하지는 않더라도
서로 어색하지 않기를
서로 외면하지 않기를
서로 상처 주지 않기를

# On the Way to There

This is a way I have to go this year.
Which way to go?

I'm going that way,
For I hope there's nothing to be angry about.

I'm going that way,
For I hope you have no regrets
I'm going that way,
For may there be no sorrow!

Who will I meet along the way?

Though we don't love each other,
I hope not to bother each other,
Nor to turn away from each other,
Nor to hurt each other.

# 쉼터 가는 길에서

겨울 저녁에 쉼터를 걷다 보면
숲속 교실 너머에
전나무 겹겹이 깔려있고
검은 바위 비스듬히
썩은 나무들 쓰러져 있고

한 굽이 더 오르면
저 아래 마을까지 보이네
저쪽 소나무밭 돌아가면
버섯 마을로 이어진다는데

차가운 산바람이 내려오니
저절로 걸음이 멈추어지네

저 아래 마을에서 누군가 올라오네
되돌아서 내려가 보아야지
누가 오는지 살펴보아야지

# On the Way to a Rest Area

At a forest on a winter evening,
Brown leaves are layered
Beyond the fir trees of the woods classroom,
Rotten trees are leaning against a black rock.

If I go up and turn one more heel,
I can see the town far below.

If I go back to the pine field,
It leads to a mushroom village.

The cold woods wind is coming down,
So I stop walking for a while.
Because in the village below.
I see someone coming up .

I'll have to go back and see,
I'll watch who's coming up.

# 새벽 망설임

새벽에 한 번 깨어났을 때
창가에 빛이 없더니

잠시 후 두 번째 깨어나니
창문에 빛이 비추네요

창문을 살짝 열어보니
낙엽 사이에 여린 눈발이 보이고
돌 틈에 차가운 서리가 보이네요

여전히 밖에 나서기는 망설여져요
어제 많이 걷지도 않았는데
다리가 피곤해지고

새벽에 눈과 서리를 보아서인지
다리에 피곤이 오네요

# Hesitation at Dawn

When I wake up once in the morning,
There is no sunlight in the window.

After a while, I wake up for the second time.
Light is shining through the window;
I open the window slightly.

Between the leaves I see soft snow.
Between the stones, I see cold frost.

I'm still hesitant to go out.
Because I did not walk much yesterday,
My legs feel tired.
Because I saw snow and frost at dawn,
My legs have been tired.

# 북극성 찾기

밤하늘은 검어서인지
아무 소리도 들리지 않아요

동쪽 오리론 별자리는
가까이 오는지 뚜렷한데

동북 방향 북두칠성은
멀어져 가는지 흐릿하고
북극성은 짐작만 할 뿐이죠

터골마을 산꼭대기에
북극성이 있어야 하는데

그 자리는 찾았는데도
희미한 자국도 보이지 않네요

오늘 밤에는 어디로 갔을까
오늘 밤 북극성은 보이지 않아요

# Where Is the North Star?

Because the night sky is black,
I can't hear anything.

The Hunter of the eastern side,
It's coming close and getting clear.

The Big Dipper of the northeast side,
It's going far away and getting blurry.

Where can I see the North Star?
There must be above the mountain.

Though I find the place of the star,
I can't even see a faint mark,
Where does it go tonight in Tugol Village?

# 이른 밤에 서리 내리고

차갑고 차가운 밤이라서
별빛도 살짝 얼어버려서
거의 빛을 내보이지 않네

겨우 손으로 더듬어 보면서
손가락 접으며 셀 정도이네

하나 둘 셋
그리고 넷 다섯 여섯

갑자기 저 아래 밭이랑에서
하얀 별들이 반짝거리는데

가만히 다가가서 살펴보니
벌써 서리가 뿌옇게 내렸네

# The Frost Early at Night

Because it's a cold and cold night,
Even starlight freezes slightly,
Almost no light in the sky.

Groping stars with my hands,
I fold my fingers and begin to count,
One, two, three,
Four, five, and six.

Suddenly, in the furrow below the field
White stars twinkle and twinkle.

I come closer and look at the twinkling,
The frost has already fallen.

# 뿌연 미세먼지

오늘까지 3일 동안이나
뿌연 미세먼지 자욱하네

아침에는 햇살을 가려서
외출을 망설이게 하더니

낮에도 시가지를 가려서
차 창문 열기가 어렵고

저녁까지 하늘을 가려서
이른 퇴근길로 이어지네

오늘 밤 늦게라도
빗방울이라도 떨어진다면
내일 아침에는
벚나무 줄기가 드러나겠지

오늘 밤 늦게라도
밤비에 살짝 젖게 되기를

# The Grey Hazy Dust

For three days until today,
It's grey with thick dust.

The sun shades in the morning,
And I hesitate to go out.

Covering the street during the day,
It's difficult to open the car window.

Covering the sky until evening,
It's leading to an early going home.

Even late at tonight,
If a little raindrop falls down,
Cherry buds will appear in the morning.

Even late at tonight,
May the rain wet the buds!

# 눈 내리는 아파트

왜 그런지 거실 커튼을 걷어보고 싶었지
왜 그런지 안쪽 창문을 열어보고 싶었지

투명한 덧문 밖으로
주차장 가로등이 보이네

여태까지 밤하늘에는
눈발이 휘날리고 있었네

앙상한 벚나무 가지 아래로
주차된 차들 지붕으로

단지 사이 연결하는 좁은 길도
하얀 빛깔로 덮여있으니

아무도 지나지 않았나보다
아니 밤에 눈이 덮었나보다

# The Snowy Apartment

For some reason,
I will open the curtains in the livingroom.
For some reason,
I will open the inside window in the room.

Out of clear window,
I see the lights of a parking lot.

So far in the night sky,
The snow is fluttering,
Under the bare cherry branches,
On the roofs of parked cars.

The sidewalk between apartment blocks
Is covered with white color.

No one seems to have passed.
It must have been snowing at night.

# 밤에 내리는 눈

창문을 조금 열고서는
가만히 손을 내밀어 보면은

손바닥 언저리를 빙글 돌아서
바로 저리로 날아가네요

손을 살살 흔들어 보면서
눈을 잡아보기를
눈에 닿아보기를
창문을 조금 더 열어보아요

한동안 눈이 더 날리겠지요

새벽까지 내려주기를
아침에 나가서 만져보기를

# Snow Falling in the Night Sky

Opening the window slightly

I quietly hold out my hand.

The snow turns around

The palm of my hand

And is flying right there.

While gently waving my hand,

Trying to touch the snowball,

I open the window a little wide.

It may be snowing for a while.

It snows till dawn I hope,

Going out to touch it in the morning.

# 낙엽 밟는 소리

낙엽 쌓인 산길에
길은 보이지 않고
낙엽 밟는 소리만 들리네

가랑잎 한 걸음 밟으면
가랑잎 바스러지는 소리
푸석 푸석 푸석

잔가지 한 걸음 밟으면
잔가지 부러지는 소리
바삭 바삭 바삭

다시 뒤돌아보아도
산길은 보이지 않아요

저 아래는 산 입구이고
저 위에 샛길일 거예요

# The Rustling of Leaves

On a path of a forest full of leaves,
I can't see the way.
I can only hear the rustling of leaves.

If I take a step on the flaky leaves,
The sound of rustling leaves remains,
Crumble, crumble, crumble.

If you step on a twig fallen on a path,
The sound of breaking twig remains,
Crunchy, crunchy, crunchy.

Though I look back again,
I can't see the path of a woods.

Below is an entrance to the forest,
Above will be a byway of the forest.

# 날아가는 낙엽

갑자기 세찬 바람 불어대니
마른 나무는
휘어져 흔들리고

겨우 붙어있던 낙엽마저
우수수 휘날리고

떨어져 쌓여있던 낙엽도
뒤집혀 동그라지네요

다시 맞바람 한껏 불어대니
떨어진 낙엽은
놀라서 일어나서는

다른 낙엽을 선동하여
나뭇가지로 내치네요

# The Flying Leaves

Suddenly a strong wind blows,
Dried trees are twisting and swaying.

Even the leaves barely attached
Are falling and flowing away.

Even the fallen leaves
Are turned upside down.

The wind is blowing again,
Fallen leaves wake up in surprise;
By agitating other leaves,
And kicking the branches.

# 고라니 지나간 길

무성한 여름 산길에서
총총총 걸어가던 고라니는

문득 뒤를 돌아보고서
이내 빗살같이 사라졌는데

앙상한 겨울 산길에는
고라니가 걸어가지 않아요
고라니 흔적이 보이지 않아요

여름에 사라진 숲속에서
햇살 비추는 저 산자락에서

자기 모습을 감추고서
여기로 귀를 기울이고 있겠지

# The Path of a Water Deer

On a lush path of summer forest,
A water deer that was walking,
Suddenly looking back once,
Disappeared like a raindrop.

Now on the bare path in winter,
The water deer does not walk,
There's no trace any more.

At the foot of the distant forest,
Where it disappeared in summer

Hiding himself under the sunlight,
He's listening to here.

# 자갈 마당 코스모스

오디나무 울타리 아래인데
서쪽 그늘에 가렸는데도
깔아 놓은 자갈에 눌려서도

여기 저기 솟아오르며
여리게 자라난 코스모스는
무릎 아래까지 자라났어요

그분이 마당에 들어가실 때
주변에 잡초를 뽑아주셨지요

지난주에 한들 한들 꽃 얼굴을 내밀고
그분이 다시 마당에 나오기를 기다려요

분홍 코스모스 다섯 송이
하얀 코스모스 세 송이
그리고 빨간 코스모스 두 송이

# The Cosmos in the Gravel Yard

Under the oak fence,
Hidden in the shade of the west,
Pressed by the gravels,
Cosmos rises softly up,
Grows up to the knee.

She sometimes pulled weeds around
When she went out to the yard.

Just last week flowers faced out,
Hoping she comes back to the yard.

The flowers have been waiting for
Her to come out to the yard.

Five pink cosmoses,
Three white cosmoses,
And two red cosmoses.

# 한적한 조강 포구들

동쪽에서 한강 흘러오고
북쪽에서 임진강 흘러들어서

저 아래 서쪽 바다로 빠져나가기에
그 옛날부터 이곳 사람들은
여기를 조강이라고 부르는데

조강 흐름은 퍽이나 한적하게
김포평야와 개풍 고장을 가로지르네

남쪽 조강포구 건너가면
북쪽 관산포구 도달하는데

참으로 오랫동안이나
남쪽 조강포구 비어있고
북쪽 관산포구 한산하네

# Quiet Ports on the Jogang Riverside

In harmony with Hangang River from the east

And Imjingang River from the north,

The joining is flowing to the westward sea.

The flow has been called Jogang River

By residents nearby since long long times.

The river has been quietly crossing

Gimpo fields of the southern part

And Gaepoong province of the northern.

Crossing from the south of Jogang Port

Arrives at the north of Gwansan Port.

However, for a long time,

The south of Jogang Port is empty,

The north of Gwansan Port is quiet.

# 그곳을 지나가면서
Passing the Way There

## 심재황 지음

발 행 처 · 도서출판 **청어**
발 행 인 · 이영철
영　　업 · 이동호
홍　　보 · 천성래
기　　획 · 남기환
편　　집 · 방세화
디 자 인 · 이수빈 | 김영은
제작이사 · 공병한
인　　쇄 · 두리터

등　　록 · 1999년 5월 3일
(제321-3210002510019990000063호)

1판 1쇄 발행 · 2022년 6월 30일

주소 · 서울특별시 서초구 남부순환로 364길 8-15 동일빌딩 2층
대표전화 · 02-586-0477
팩시밀리 · 0303-0942-0478

홈페이지 · www.chungeobook.com
E-mail · ppi20@hanmail.net
ISBN · 979-11-6855-048-3(03810)